62
JS

DEATH IN THE SUN

First published in this edition May 1945

MADE AND PRINTED IN GREAT BRITAIN BY C. J. COUSLAND & SONS LTD., EDINBURGH

DEATH IN THE SUN

by

G. D. H. & M. COLE

VALLANCEY PRESS LIMITED

Three · Temple Avenue · London · EC · 4

DEATH IN THE SUN

I

"IT really is beautiful here. Thank you so much for bringing me, James, dear," said Mrs. Warrender, leaning back and sipping her glass of very mild Portuguese white wine with a smile of pleased satisfaction. "I've never known a place where it was so beautifully warm at night without being a bit too hot in the daytime."

She turned to look through the open loggia behind her at the still waters of the Bay of Funchal, the curving line of lights that marked the mole of the tiny harbour, the spangled black hill on the farther side of the bay, and the garish illumination of a liner at anchor.

"Umph!" said her son, with a grunt and a creak of his dress-shirt. "It was hot enough down in the town this morning, anyhow."

"I'm sure it must have been, dear," his mother said. "It's too bad you should have to go down there in such horrid stuffy places. But it's lucky for me, because if you didn't we shouldn't be getting this lovely holiday. And it's quite cool now, isn't it?"

"Cool enough, but damnably noisy," James Warrender answered. He and his mother were sitting on the very edge of the Grand Hotel's open dance-and-dining-room, finishing their dinner at one of the tables which encircled the dance floor. The soft evening breeze of Madeira came up to them from the sea below,

Mrs. Warrender gazed happily at the dancers swirling past their table.

" Oh, James ! " she exclaimed. " Look how beautifully those two are dancing ! They're from the party that came in to dinner, aren't they ? "

The couple in question were doing a kind of exhibition display. The man was about twenty-five, tall, beautifully proportioned, with short curling black hair, a sun-tanned face, and a profile which was certainly in the first photographic rank. His partner, only three or four inches shorter, slender and aquiline, made in colour a perfect contrast. Her pale golden hair was only the merest shade darker in tone than her faintly sun-flushed skin, and against his evening clothes her sheath of silver lamé shone like a moon. But it was not the colour combination so much as the perfect timing and finish of their dancing that arrested attention. They moved like a single creature, executing complicated manoeuvres amid the other dancers without a second's mistiming or hesitation.

" They *can* dance ! " Mrs. Warrender repeated, with a sigh of satisfaction.

" Well, she ought to be able to, at any rate," James said, with a faint hint of sourness. " She's the dancing and swimming instructress from Wright's Hotel. I wonder they let her out to come and show off at a one-horse place like this."

" Perhaps it's her evening off," said Mrs. Warrender dreamily. " It must be nice for her if she can get taken out herself sometimes. Do you know who the young man is, dear ? He's wonderfully good-looking."

" Not an idea. By his looks and his clothes he must come from Wright's too. It's the only place where gilded youths

of his type stay. Or perhaps he's landed off a summer cruise
—no, I forgot it's to-morrow the *Armadilla* comes in. D'you
mind if I leave you, mother ? I want to go through those
papers properly again, before I go to bed. I ought to know
what's in them by to-morrow, and I can't attend to anything
with this racket going on. You won't mind, will you ? Get
yourself some coffee, or a drink, or anything else you like."

" Of course not, dear. I shall be perfectly happy ; I don't
want anything at all," said his mother, and leaned back in
her chair while the waiter cleared away the débris, looking
with half-shut eyes at the dancers, and thinking how lucky
she was, at sixty-five, to be enjoying this holiday in Madeira
and how entirely unexpected it had been, even though it did
mean that poor James had to go and argue with Portuguese
in stuffy offices in the heat.

Mrs. Warrender was not at all wealthy. Her tiny income
would certainly not have stretched to a holiday in Madeira
had not James, in his capacity of private enquiry agent, been
given a lucrative if tiresome commission which involved his
going out to Madeira and spending a great deal of time
interviewing shipping and wine companies. Fortunately, the
client was lavish, and James who was always generous—
even if he did sometimes fidget and demand his money's
worth—had announced that the fees would easily cover both
their expenses, if they shut up the house in Hampstead for
the time.

So there she was, after a voyage of delirious excitement
for a lady who had never been out of Europe, sitting on an
almost open terrace at nine in the evening by an almost
tropical sea. She lapsed into a reverie.

But not for long. By an accident which none of the Grand

Hotel's usually efficient staff had noticed, the people at the table nearest hers had, in rising, knocked over a beaker of salad dressing which was slowly spreading in a greasy pool over the floor. Into this pool swept the girl from Wright's and her partner, in a magnificent sea-gull swoop—and instantly skidded.

They made a great effort to recover themselves, but they were going too fast and with too much abandon. After cannoning off the table from which the oil had come, they shot straight into that of the Warrenders, and sent it crashing on its side. The girl tripped over Mrs. Warrender's feet and fell helter-skelter into the chair which James had been occupying. The young man, graceful even in disaster, dropped back on his heels and came to rest, almost in a squatting position, with his arms encircling Mrs. Warrender, chair and all, and his dark eyes looking up into her face with a comic expression of dismay.

" Good heavens ! " he exclaimed, rising swiftly. " What clumsiness ! I'm so sorry. I do hope we haven't hurt you much."

" Not a bit," said Mrs. Warrender, while the girl extricated herself from the chair. " It wasn't your fault at all. Somebody spilt some oil on the floor."

" Why, so they did," said the young man, in great relief. " That lets me out a bit—except that anybody who could dance at all oughtn't to slip on a patch of grease."

" But if you're dancing the way you two were—not just walking, but moving so beautifully—you couldn't possibly help it. It was so lovely to watch you," said Mrs. Warrender eagerly.

" Oh, but how charming of you ! " the young man said.

" I do hope we haven't spilt anything that matters."

" Nothing at all, thank you," said Mrs. Warrender.
" There wasn't anything there to spill."

" Oh, but there ought to be ! You will have a drink with
me, won't you ? It's the least I can do, after throwing partners
and tables all over you. Some champagne ? " Mrs. Warrender
shook her head. " But you must ! " And, turning to the girl
in silver, " *You* tell her she ought to, Florence."

" Do, please," said the girl. She had a low, pleasant
voice, though possibly she was not as young as she appeared
to be at a distance. She was beautifully *soignée*, and the lift
of her head was clear and even defiant ; but anybody who
looked close could detect a weary, indeed almost a wary,
look in her eyes, as though life were beginning to press hard.
Mrs. Warrender glanced at her with a sudden feeling of
sympathy, but shook her head again.

" But, please—oh, I'm sorry. This is somebody's chair,
isn't it ? " the girl said.

" No, indeed. I'm all by myself."

" But you mustn't be ! That's all wrong," said the young
man ; " and on so lovely an evening too. It makes people
come and bump into your table and send it flying. You are
sure you're not hurt ? Florence didn't tear your stockings
with her new sharpened heels, did she ? " And, as Mrs.
Warrender smiled and shook her head, " Then you really
must have a drink with us. Look, we're all abandoned ; our
friends have swep' out and gone to the bar and we've got
no one to play with. Don't you like champagne ? Will you
have a veesky-soda ? I believe that's the correct drink for
modern matrons, isn't it ? "

" I really won't have anything like that, thank you,"

Mrs. Warrender smiled. " But if you would like me to—I *would* enjoy a little coffee——"

" Splendid ! " said the young man, and clapped his hands for a waiter.

She found him charming, like something out of a very pleasant dream, as he stood inclining his shapely dark head. With the tail of her always maternal eye, she considered and approved his companion.

" Surely you are not here all by yourself ? " he asked when the waiter had come and he had secured a chair.

" Oh, no. My son is with me——"

" How nice for him," the young man replied softly.

Mrs. Warrender, who in her far-off girlhood had been famous for her dimples, produced an unexpected one at the corner of her cheek. " He was dining with me, only he had to go and do some work. You're not staying here, are you ? "

" No. We're at Wright's," he answered. " This is Miss Florence Truman, and my name's Jeremy Haydon. We've come here for a night out, away from all the financiers and colonial governors at Wright's. There are two others with us, Terry Gordon and Clare Ferrers. I'll introduce them directly ; but as I said they've gone off to the bar. And you ? "

" Our name's Warrender. My son is James Warrender."

" I say ! You don't mean *the* James Warrender, do you ? The man who's a great big private detective and agent— whom everybody's heard of ? "

Mrs. Warrender nodded in pride, thinking what a pity it was that James couldn't be there to hear. He would never believe it if she told him ; he always said, when she tried to pass on compliments, that she must have misheard and that nobody ever said nice things of him behind his back. James was cynical about the world.

" But, in that case . . . you must be the wonderful woman who is back of him, who always gets the hunches——"

" Oh, no ! That's not true at all," Mrs. Warrender said, hoping now that James would *not* suddenly appear. " I don't have anything to do with his work."

" But, you see, I've got a sort of uncle—isn't it extra-ordinary that everybody you meet always knows somebody else ? I know that sounds silly, but you know what I mean."

" Like me knowing your sister," Florence Truman put in.

" Exactly." (But Mrs. Warrender noticed a cloud cross his face, and felt rather than saw, that Miss Truman had noticed it also.)

" As I was saying, my uncle is a Magistrate somewhere in London, and I'm quite certain I remember him telling me about a burglary in Hampstead at the house of *the* James Warrender, where he—Mr. Warrender, I mean—hadn't been able to do anything about it, but his mother solved it and caught the criminal and all."

" Oh, but that's ridiculous," Mrs. Warrender said, dimpling again. " It was only, you see, that I happened to know Gladys."

" Gladys ! Who's Gladys ? Oh, do tell us."

" Why, Gladys was our maid. You see," said Mrs. Warrender, " I went away for the week-end, and when I came back I found James very cross, because all the silver had been stolen in the night. And he said Gladys had been woken by the burglar and had gone and screamed at the front door instead of calling him or anything. But I knew Gladys wouldn't have done a silly thing like stand and scream at the front door—unless she knew that somebody was getting away through the back door. So I told the inspector to go and see Gladys's young man, and he did, and found he was the thief. But—no, no," as they began to laugh and applaud, " that wasn't being a detective at all. It was only that I happened to know something about Gladys and of course James didn't."

" Well, I think it's superb," Jeremy Haydon began. " Hi ! " he broke off, as his eye caught some people in the distance. " Hi ! Come over here, you two. Meet Mrs. Warrender, mother of the great detective, and a four-flusher on her own. Mrs. Warrender—Miss Ferrers, Terry Gordon. Have a drink, you-all."

" Pleased to meet you," Terry Gordon said, without interest. Mrs. Warrender thought that she liked this pair much less than her previous companions. The young man was sleek, fair, and sinuous. He had a long narrow head, eyes set too close together, and a sulky mouth with a drooping lower lip. The girl was young, but what James would have called " hard-boiled." Her hair was waved tight and close ; she had long jade earrings, eyebrows plucked and replaced at an impossible angle, and blood-red nails ending in sharp points. And she twitched. Her eyelids twitched, and her mouth twitched, and her fingers fidgetted and tapped on anything within reach.

" Of course I want a drink," she said, motioning young Gordon to find her a chair. " But not here, in this lousy place. Let's get off and pub-crawl."

"It's nicer here," Jeremy said. "Cooler. Besides, we can't pub-crawl unless Terry's got any cash, and I don't suppose he has." Terry shook his head emphatically.

"Oh, are you broke? What a curse. Can't you borrow on your expectations or something?"

Again the cloud crossed Jeremy's face, and Florence Truman shifted suddenly on her chair.

Mrs. Warrender took a small decision, and rose to her feet. "I must go and see what my son's doing," she said. "Good-night, Mr. Haydon; good-night, Miss Truman. And thank you so much for a pleasant evening."

"Thank you," Jeremy said. "And, I say, won't you return the call some time? Come over to Wright's to-morrow morning and bathe, won't you? About eleven. We've quite a decent bathing-pool there. And I'll find you some coconut oil."

"I bet you will," said Clare Ferrers to the company at large. "Jeremy's a perfect old woman about his bathing. Lies in the sun for hours and cooks himself by the clock both sides—ten minutes either way—basting himself like a spring chicken."

"Of course I do," said Jeremy, not at all put out. "Madeira sun's fierce, and I don't want to go home covered with sores, whatever anybody else may do. But you will come, won't you?" to Mrs. Warrender.

"I don't know that I will bathe, thank you," Mrs. Warrender said. "I bathe here early, and I think that is enough for an old lady. But I should like very much to come and call on you both sometime. And now I really must say good-night." She extricated herself, but not too soon to hear Clare Ferrers remark, "Well, you have got catholic tastes, haven't you? What is it you're vamping now, gigolo?"

Upstairs she found her son, his work finished, wondering whether filial duty demanded that he should return again to the dance-room, and very relieved to find that it would not be necessary.

"Hullo!" he said. "Had a nice time?"

"Very, thank you, dear," his mother replied. "I made the acquaintance of that young couple—you know, the girl you said was a dancing-instructress at Wright's, and the young man. His name's Jeremy Haydon; he's a charming boy. . . . Why, James, do you know him?" For his brow had knitted in a surprised scowl.

"Not him. But I know about him, a bit. He's the son of old Haydon, the banker, who died a year or two ago. He's got a sister who married that rotter Maurice Benoni. That's how I came to know about it, because Haydon asked me to look into Benoni. So I did, and I didn't find anything, though I never had any doubt that there was something shady about him. But I never heard any more of it, so maybe it turned out all right. Is this chap staying at Wright's?"

"Yes. Why?"

"It's what I should expect. Money to burn and nothing to do. At least I don't suppose he's got control of it yet, from what the old man told me, but I dare say he can drink himself to death on his expectations."

"I thought he was such a nice boy. I didn't care for some of his friends, though. There was a girl—quite pretty, but, oh, so disagreeable and restless. She made me quite jumpy," Mrs. Warrender said.

" Drugs, probably. They're a sodden lot in these places,"
said James. " Well, how about a spot of bed, mother ? "

" The big German boat's gone," said Mrs. Warrender,
looking out of the window towards the bay.

" Left half an hour ago," James said. " The British cruise
comes in to-morrow. Well, good-night, ma mère."

II

"LOOK, James, isn't it curious, the way people turn up!" Mrs. Warrender, eating her breakfast on the terrace in the sun two days later, was fluttering in a pleased way over an envelope that had just been delivered by hand. She was very happy this morning; she had had a perfect bathe, and had even, with the encouragement of an amiable Portuguese gentleman, ventured into the open sea beyond the pool. And now here was a note, and from Wright's hotel, asking her and James to pay a visit.

"Lang? Who's Lang? Pernicia Lang—what a name!" James said.

"It isn't Pernicia, dear, it's Persis, only her writing is always so bad."

"Well, who's Pernicious Lang, then?" James grunted.

"Oh, James dear, you know Dr. Lang—Hubert Lang. It's him and his wife. They're staying at Wright's—I'm sure I don't know how they came to know we were here."

"Oh, them," James looked at the letter again. "Well, I can't go to-day. I don't want to waste all the morning."

"No, dear, I know you don't. But I thought, perhaps, if I went round in the morning and had a little chat with them you might spare time to come over to lunch. They would be so pleased to see you, if you're not too busy. And, after all, you must have lunch somewhere, mustn't you?"

"Um-m. Well, perhaps I might," said James graciously.

"I'll just run along and tell them now," his mother said.

So it happened that, at midday, Mrs. Elizabeth Warrender was sitting, in a chair of bright steel and scarlet canvas, alongside Mrs. Persis Lang amid the plumbago and hibiscus of the gardens of Wright's Hotel, looking out over the bay.

The bathing-pool, where Dr. Lang and his son and daughter were disporting themselves, lay just below them at the bottom of the cliffs ; but the two ladies had not bathed.

" I bathe before my breakfast," Mrs. Lang was saying in a voice that would have carried easily to the bathing-pool and beyond ; " and that's enough for me. I don't fancy lying about there in the sun with all those young things and everybody looking at me and calculating exactly how big a splash I'll make when I go in." She gave a huge reverberating guffaw, which shook her all over.

Mrs. Hubert Lang accepted the occasional inconveniences of her size with loud and cheerful comment, secure in the fact that her personality easily dominated her family, and that her very comfortable income not only served to give them holidays at the best hotel in Funchal, but had also raised her husband—a little hurried and hesitant man whom nature had obviously designed for a struggling G.P.—to the comparative dignity of a practice in Harley Street. Her two children appeared to be both proud and fond of her, though Mrs. Warrender did sometimes, when she allowed herself to entertain so uncharitable a thought, wonder whether Jocelyn Lang ever shivered in anticipation when her mother's figure came and sat down beside her—even more, whether any of Jocelyn's young men ever shivered.

" But that's no reason why you shouldn't have a bathe, my dear," Mrs. Lang continued. " Are you sure you won't ? Geoffrey and Jocelyn would be delighted to see you—they're in and out of the water all the time, and they're pretty nearly making Hubert a duck between them."

" No, really, thank you," Mrs. Warrender said. " I've got so used to having just my early bathe that I don't want another. And you seem to have to do such a lot of lying in the sun and rubbing yourself with oil ; I'm sure I should do it wrong and get a bad burn—and it isn't as though it was any use to *me* to have a nice brown back——"

B

" Well, that's true, too."

"—Besides, it is so pleasant here, looking at the sea and your lovely garden."

" Let's look at a bit more of it, shall we ? " said Mrs. Lang, beginning to heave herself out of her chair. " They've really done it pretty well. It's worth seeing and though I'm large I'm not immovable yet. Besides, I shall have to go down to the pool sooner or later, to drag the others up to lunch. It wouldn't ever occur to them to come out of the water if I didn't fetch them. And I think you ought to see our pool ; it's really rather prettily arranged. So let's walk down through the gardens, and we'll call Hubert out of the water and have a nice John Collins before lunch."

" I met such a charming young man from your hotel the other evening," said Mrs. Warrender, stopping to bury her appreciative nose in a great bush of frangipanni. " He was over dining in ours with some friends. He said his name was Jeremy Haydon." Mrs. Lang nodded in qualified approval.

" *I* think he's a nice boy," she said, " though I can't say as much for some of his friends here, and they do racket about a lot and drink like fishes. Hubert keeps on worrying that they will pick up Geoffrey and do him some harm ; but what I say is, if Geoffrey's going to be a fool, a fool he'll be and much better do it here, where he can get away and forget all about it in a month, than in London or somewhere like that. Not that it's very likely ; Geoffrey's much too like Hubert—afraid of getting his underpants wet.

" Young Haydon's got really pretty manners, that's what I like about him," she continued after a pause. " He may be a ne'er-do-well—dare say he is—but he doesn't treat a fat old woman as if she was just an ugly bit of furniture left over from last spring-cleaning. And whatever you may say of him, he's not a snob ; he's just as nice to the hotel dancing-partner as he is to any of his own friends—and I dare say she could do with it, poor girl."

" Doesn't she have a very pleasant time, then ? " Mrs. Warrender enquired.

" Not too good. Some of the old wretches here," Mrs. Lang bellowed almost in the ear of a very frail old gentleman who was climbing shakily down a short flight of steps, " think they've bought the world because they're paying twice as much for their drinks as they would anywhere else. And old Lewis—that's the manager, and a Jew if ever I saw one —is a skinflint and a bully. I've heard him ticking off the girl once or twice in a way that's made my blood boil. But young Haydon's always charming to her."

" He's very good-looking," Mrs. Warrender said. " He must look beautiful in the water."

" Well, you'll be able to judge of that yourself in a minute," said Mrs. Lang, turning into a steep path which appeared to lead direct to the pool, " in the water or out of it. He's pretty certain to be down at the pool ; he generally spends most of the morning there, swimming or sunbathing." She paused to chuckle. " He's very particular about his tan, I must say, and goes about it most scientifically. His friends teased him about it so much—though I must say the result's worth looking at in my opinion—that he generally goes and lies by himself on a bit of rock and won't talk to anybody. Matter of fact, I seem to remember seeing him there early this morning, when we came down. So perhaps he won't be there now."

" Is he a good swimmer ? " Mrs. Warrender asked.

" Beautiful. We'll have to get him to dive for you, if he's there, before we go up to lunch." By now they had arrived at the pool, a great shining expanse of clear green water, flanked by terraced rocks on which various half-clad figures lay bathing in the sun. " Geoffrey ! "

" Adsum !" A young man in a black bathing slip climbed out of the pool at their feet.

" Where's your father ? "

"In the sea. Trying to climb on a rubber horse," Geoffrey chuckled.

"Call him out, will you? It's time, if we're to have a drink before lunch. And, Geoffrey!" as the young man turned to obey. "Is Jeremy Haydon down, do you know? Mrs. Warrender wants him to dive for her."

"Oh, but I didn't mean——" Mrs. Warrender went faintly pink, but neither took any notice of her.

"I think so. Yes, that's him, over there on the rock. I haven't seen him in the water since I came down, so I dare say he'll be about ready for another dip. Go and ask him, won't you, Mrs. Warrender, while I whistle up father."

And Geoffrey sprang off, with a cry of "Hi! Jos! Come and haul the old man in," while Mrs. Lang waddled purposefully in the direction of the pavilion.

Left to herself, Mrs. Warrender found herself moving slowly, and not without a tiny tremor of excitement, in the direction of the solitary figure lying on its face on a brilliant orange mattress of rubber. After all, he *had* invited her to come and see him, and he was always charming to old ladies, so that he wouldn't be rude to her, even if he did prefer to be alone. Perhaps he might even be pleased that she had come. She quickened her steps a little, glad to be going to meet Jeremy Haydon again.

He was lying all alone on the farthest of the rock terraces. He was lying at full length, his head pillowed on his arms, and nothing on his finely shaped body but a pair of bright blue bathing-trunks, which showed up perfectly the deep bronze tan of his skin. Nothing of his head was visible; it was concealed by one of the huge striped Madeiran straw hats, which covered his shoulders as well, and was presumably protecting him from sunstroke. He lay very still, not moving a muscle at her approach. Was it wise, her maternal mind wondered, to lie so fast asleep in the full sub-tropical sun?

She stood looking at him for a moment, noticing subconsciously a faint tinge of green in the bronze of his back, and wondering what trick of light could have caused it.

It seemed a shame to disturb him ; he looked so peaceful. But it would be nice to talk to him a little, and perhaps he, too, would like a drink before lunch. And, anyway, she was sure he oughtn't to go on sleeping there in the glare. So she called his name, softly at first, and then louder, " Mr. Haydon ! " but he did not stir.

Suddenly, as she looked, her heart gave a sickening leap, and the bright blue sea turned momentarily to a greyish-black. For a second she stood, with her eyes painfully screwed up, verifying what she had seen. Then she turned, trembling, back in the direction of the pool. For she had seen flies walking on his bare skin—and he had not even moved to brush them away.

Her heart thumping, she walked as quickly as she could back to the pool and there was fortunate enough to find her host, just out of the water.

" Dr. Lang ! Could you come a moment, please ? I think —perhaps—Mr. Haydon may be ill over there." She spoke in a low voice—even in panic, Mrs. Warrender could never have brought herself to shout.

" He's lying so still," she explained, following the doctor. " It looks—he might have fainted or had a sunstroke."

" Righto. We'll see," said Dr. Lang cheerfully. " Now you mention it, I haven't seen him about much to-day, and it isn't too safe to lie too long in this sun." By now he had reached the young man, and whipped the hat from his head, disclosing the dark hair and the crooked elbows. Certainly he had not been in the water for some time ; his hair was perfectly dry.

Dr. Lang knelt down beside him in his dripping suit, and laid a hand on his back. Immediately his face changed, and he half-lifted the limp figure and slipped a hand under the shoulder. For a second he kept it there, then turned to Mrs.

Warrender. In a peremptory bark, which she would hardly
have recognised, he said, " Fetch Geoffrey, will you ? Quick,
please."

.   .   .   .   .   .

How Mrs. Warrender got back she hardly knew, but
somehow she did, and managed, after some delay, to extract
Geoffrey Lang from the dressing-box into which he had
disappeared.

" My *dear* ! " Mrs. Lang, who had been a surprised
spectator of her frenzied search for Geoffrey, boomed suddenly in her ear. " Are you ill ? You've gone as white as
a sheet. Is anything—*what's the matter* ? "

" I don't know ! . . . It's Mr. Haydon. I *must* go and
see ! " Shaking all over, Mrs. Warrender hurried on ; and
the large lady followed her at a slower pace. The sound of
her voice had disturbed a number of the sunbathers, who
began to sit up and look round, and there was a slow drift
of the more active among them in the same direction.

When Mrs. Warrender got back to the rock, she found
that Dr. Lang and his son had turned young Haydon over,
and the former was still on his knees making an examination.
He raised a hand to keep her back, but she paid no attention,
approaching as near as she could to the boy. He lay on his
back now, with his eyes wide open and staring straight into
the sun, and the greenish tinge of the bronze tan was far
more noticeable in his face. Mrs. Warrender had never seen
anyone quite that colour before, and for a second she closed
her eyes.

" Is he . . . ? " she said, hoping against hope that she did
not know the answer to her question.

" Yes. He's dead," Dr. Lang almost snapped, seeming
not to realise to whom he was speaking. Then he glanced
up and saw the slow trek of people approaching. " Good
Lord ! " he said. " Geoffrey, go and keep that lot back, and

send somebody for the manager quick. We don't want anyone here. No, Mrs. Warrender," in a gentler, though still preoccupied tone, " it's no good your coming. There's nothing to be done for him."

" But surely," Mrs. Warrender protested faintly, " there must be something—aren't you going to try and bring him round? He may be only in a bad faint."

" Good God!" the doctor suddenly barked. " He's been dead for hours, I tell you! He's as cold as a stone, except where the sun's got at him. Been lying here all night, most likely."

" Oh!" said Mrs. Warrender, and swayed.

" Hold up," said Geoffrey Lang. " Look here, sit down a bit." He guided her to a niche in the rock, where she sank down with her hands over her eyes to shut out the sight and the understanding. " *Oh!* " she said, as the tears came seeping through her hands. " The poor boy. The *poor* boy."

III

IT seemed hours before she could endure to remove her hands from her face, and look again at the rock at her feet, and the still blue sea, with the white awnings of the fishing-boats making a pattern on the horizon. For some reason, the thought of Jeremy Haydon's dead body lying out all night, and for half the day, uncared for and unnoticed by those around him, struck at her heart even more deeply than his death, though that was shock enough. How *could* people, she raged to herself, how could they be so cold and uninterested as not even to have seen that he had not moved for hours, not even to have noticed that he had not been for a swim, not even to have asked him to come and dive for them? For, if they had, if somebody had come over to speak to him—Dr. Lang might have been wrong, and it might not have been too late. They might have done something for him, revived him, before he had got so cold—so cold that even the Madeira sun could not warm him through the chill. And then, suddenly, a fresh realisation overcame her that Jeremy Haydon, the lithe dancer who had overset her table little more than thirty-six hours before and had squatted on his heels apologising in his nice voice and asking her to come and bathe with him, would never dance or upset anything again, and once more the easy tears of old age burnt her cheeks.

She roused herself, at the sound of harsh argumentative voices, and opened her eyes again. Nothing had changed very much since she had shut them. The body of Jeremy Haydon still lay sprawled on its orange mattress on the rock, against a cascade of red bougainvillea—curious that she had not noticed that before—which was falling down from the cliff-edges. But a number of new people had appeared. One, a short dark man with a fleshy nose, and an obviously corseted figure, was making most of the noise which had aroused her. He was shouting directions at two or three men in long white coats and black trousers, and at the same time, it would appear, conducting an argument with the doctor. Possibly he was the manager of the hotel. She sat up, in order to see better what was happening, and as she did so her foot struck against a small object that was lying on the rock, at which she automatically turned to look. She was not four feet from the mattress on which the body was lying.

" It's no use trying to bully me," Dr. Lang was saying with a truculence that she never expected to hear from him. " I'm not going to give you any opinion until I've had time to make a proper examination, and I can't do that in this blazing sun without any clothes on. You get him to his own room, and I'll come up directly and look into it properly."

" He hasn't got any room," the manager said, " not that he's paid for. It's more than a fortnight now since he's paid me a penny for his keep or the drinks he and his friends mopped up. If I hadn't believed he's got friends and money in the background somewhere, I'd have told him to clear out. Now he's dead——"

" Yes, he's dead ; and if you think that is a way to behave when a guest of yours dies in your bathing-pool, I'll soon inform you that you're mistaken ! " Dr. Lang stormed. " Get him up, I tell you, and I'll tell you directly everything you need to know. If you don't and if you say another word, I'll lodge a complaint with the British Consul in half an hour from now. Get a move on, I tell you ! Where's your stretcher ? Well, then, put him on. You needn't handle him like glass, man ; you can't do him any harm now."

With excruciating slowness, like the dreariest of educational films, the white-coated men produced a stretcher, and on to it loaded the corpse. Slowly they moved back along the rocks ; and Dr. Lang heaved a sigh, and reclaimed the large bathing towel which his wife was dutifully holding for him.

" Have to get back quick and dress," he observed. " Can't do anything like this. Mrs. Warrender all right ? Good God ! " with a sudden change of tone. " What are you doing with that ? Put it down quick ! Where'd you find it ? "

Mrs. Warrender dropped, as if it were red-hot, the small object against which her foot had struck. " It was just here, by me," she said feebly. " I touched it, and picked it up. I'm sorry ; I didn't know it mattered."

" It's a hypodermic," exclaimed Dr. Lang. " Better let me have it, and not touch it again. You see," he swallowed hard, " one can't tell how he died. People don't die like that, from lying out all night, when there isn't even any sun. And a hypodermic syringe—an injection—that might tell us." .

" Oh !" said Mrs. Warrender, surrendering the syringe. " Perhaps you'd better have that little bottle too." She pointed to one a yard or two away, which had rolled into the shadow of the rock-wall. " It looks like coconut oil, and he told me that he always had plenty of it, so I suppose it may have been his."

" Yes, I'll take it." Dr. Lang dived and secured it with his handkerchief. " Thanks, m'dear," turning to his wife. " I'd better get up. Can't tell how long this will take, but I'll be along as soon as I can. You'll be all right ? Better start lunch without waiting for me."

Mrs. Warrender and Mrs. Lang, clinging together like two stricken madonnas, crawled back to the hotel, where they found Mrs. Warrender's son, who had just witnessed the body of Jeremy Haydon being carried through the hotel door, and had heard of the tragedy. He was, in fact, already putting two and two together, rather callously, the Langs thought.

" There doesn't seem much doubt," he informed them, when they were seated in the dining-room, " that the young fellow committed suicide."

There was a shower of startled exclamations. " What ? But why on earth ? "

" How do you know ? " said Geoffrey Lang.

" Lord, what a blow ! " said his sister.

Mrs. Lang said, " Nonsense ! That nice cheerful boy kill himself. I don't believe it for a single minute."

Mrs. Warrender, after her first cry, said nothing at all. She was remembering Dr. Lang's face when he spoke to her after the body had gone. He had seemed oddly worried ; had he thought then that something was wrong ? But surely —to kill oneself one must be terribly unhappy. Could he— Jeremy—have been so unhappy, and still talked to her so lightly ? Or was he—had something disastrous happened to him since ?

" It isn't nonsense, you know," James said. " I wouldn't say it if it were. And he wasn't as bright and cheerful as all that—at least he oughtn't to have been. He was getting into deep water. He'd been running up bills here for a couple of weeks and more—pretty hefty bills too—I gather he let his friends sponge on him right and left ; and I dare say they'll find he had more owing in the town. Anyway, the point is that he'd no means of paying them, as far as we know. The fellows whom he was banking with here—according to the manager—said that instructions from England were strict not to let him anticipate his allowance by more than a certain amount, and I understand, also from the manager, that he'd already got to that limit. So, you see, he was pretty well due for a showdown in a day or so. Just the sort of thing a lad like that, who'd been throwing his weight about and cutting a dash, wouldn't like to have to face."

" But then, how ? I mean, how did he do it ? " Geoffrey Lang asked.

" Oh, that. Well, you see, it wasn't a natural death. Your husband, Mrs. Lang, is quite sure of that. He's just making a final examination, and he'll probably call for a p.m. ; but he told *me* he hadn't any doubts it would turn out to be morphine poisoning. I understand somebody or other found a hypodermic just close to his body. They'll probably find he was an addict, when they come to investigate. Lots of these fly-by-night young people are. All bright and starry-eyed when they've got their dope, and heavy as lead and fretted to fiddle-strings as soon as it's worn off."

Mrs. Warrender very quietly, hoping her action would not be noticed, put down the mouthful that was choking her. It couldn't be—that bright gaiety *couldn't* be produced by drug-taking. But then, she realised sadly, quiet old ladies don't really know much about the effect of drugs.

"Added to which," James was saying, "the manager's been on to that dancing girl he brought over to our place the other night—you remember, mother, I think you were talking to them—and she's let out that the young man has seemed pretty much under the weather the last day or two. Hullo, mother, what's up?"

"You ought to be more careful what you say, James! Frightening your mother like that," said Mrs. Lang indignantly. "Here, waiter, a cognac, quickly."

Mrs. Warrender leaned back, apologising in a faint voice, though in reality it was not James's words that had startled her, but the sudden sight of a tall girl with a white, absolutely stricken face passing the doors of the dining-room. Florence Truman, at least, was not indifferent to Haydon's death. Nobody else, however, appeared to have noticed her ; and, as Dr. Lang appeared almost immediately and showed a marked disinclination to discuss the case, Mrs. Warrender was mercifully left to toy with her lunch in peace.

"Well, mother, how about getting along home?" James suggested when he had finished. "I've got a good lot of things to do, and I suggest you ought to lie down and have a rest. You look pretty played out, and you'll want to be in decent trim when you've got to give evidence."

" Oh, *no* ! I shan't, shall I ? Shall I have to ? "

" 'Fraid so, at the inquest, or whatever it is they have in this country. You see, it was you who found him. She will, won't she ? " to Dr. Lang.

" Maybe. Might be arranged. No need to bother about it now," the doctor grunted. He scribbled on a bit of paper in his pocket. " Here, Warrender, take this and get your hotel to make it up pronto, and give it to Mrs. Warrender. You take things easy," he said to her, " and don't go sitting in the sun."

" No, I won't," said Mrs. Warrender, with a faint, wilted smile. " It's—it's rather dangerous, isn't it ? "

He looked at her with a glance of comprehension, but all he said was, " Only need to be a bit careful—that's all. But you—had a shock—don't knock yourself up. Bad business, anyway."

" Dr. Lang, I don't want to ask things I shouldn't. But do you really think it was that—that he poisoned himself ? "

" 'Fraid so. From all I could see. 'Course it's not official, yet, but—bad business," said Dr. Lang again. " Nice-looking lad."

" Thank you ! But I can't—I can't believe it," Mrs. Warrender thought to herself as she passed on James's arm out of the hotel and along the cobbled, palm-lined road which she had traversed so happily three hours before.

IV

" **B**ETTER tuck yourself up and have a bit of a shut-eye, mother," said James when they had got back to the Grand Hotel and the prescription had been handed to the chemist. " No use knocking yourself up."

" No, dear. But I don't think I'll get to bed, if you don't mind," his mother said. " It's so hot in my bedroom in the afternoon, and I've got rather a headache. I think I'll just go and sit quietly in the garden."

It was not, however, the heat, but sleep, that she was afraid of. By keeping her eyes firmly open, she was just able not to see that scene on the rocks, with the blood-red bougainvillea hanging down to within a foot of the boy's head ; but once she shut them she knew that it would all come vividly back. So she made her way, with a half-knitted sock of James's, to a hard iron seat in the Grand Hotel's back garden, under an extraordinarily twisted kind of tree whose name she had never discovered. It was hot, however, even in the garden ; the knitting-needles felt sticky in her hands, and the restless lizards running to and fro dazzled her eyes. After a very little effort she laid down the knitting and fixed her gaze on the bright green fronds of a banana plantation in the distance, just by which a white sheet or garment of some sort was fluttering in the air. She kept her eyes sternly fastened on it until sheer strain forced her to close them, and when she opened them again it seemed that the white object had moved. She stared until she was certain she was right : not only had it moved, but it was still moving. It was coming straight towards her, flapping its sides—no, its wings. It was an enormous bird.

It was all rather extraordinary. She had not noticed any

gulls in Madeira, and this seemed a particularly large one—
and what was it doing in the grounds of the hotel? It was
circling about—it seemed to be looking for something. She
rather hoped it would not come near; it was such a big bird,
and in some unreasonable way it frightened her.

But it did come near. It came quite close, and then rose
straight above her head, so that she could see it perfectly
clearly; it was a fierce predatory bird with a great beak, and
it looked hungry. She gave a little shiver of fright—could it
be going to attack her? But no. With a hoarse cry it swooped
past her, just to her feet, and she screamed in sheer terror as
she realised what it was doing—tearing with a hungry beak
at something below her—something which lay naked and
defenceless on the sun-baked rock. . . .

"I beg your pardon, madam. Are you not well?"

Mrs. Warrender lifted her head with a start. No—how
ridiculous! Of course this was the hotel garden, with the
flowers and the lizards, just as usual. There was nothing else
there, no rock, no hungry bird of prey. Even the washing
had been taken from the banana-plantation; and there was
an hotel servant standing beside her seat, looking at her with
an expression of concern, and telling her, as far as she could
make out, that she was wanted on the telephone. How stupid
of her—what could she have been imagining?

She was a little surprised that there was anyone in Madeira
who could want to telephone to her; but she got up and went
obediently if rather shakily into the telephone-box.

"'Allo," she said, trying ineffectively to answer like a
foreigner.

"Is that Mrs. Warrender?" a strained voice answered
her. "Mrs. Warrender, it's Florence Truman speaking, from
Wright's Hotel. I don't know if you'll remember me——"

"Indeed I do."

"Mrs. Warrender, I'm afraid it's a lot to ask, but could
you possibly come over and see me? I'd come to you, but

I can't get away—not now. They'll be watching me . . . and I *must* talk to somebody. *Could* you ? "

" Why, of course, if you really want me . . ."

" You know what it's about," Florence Truman's went on urgently. " I can't—I daren't talk to you much on the 'phone, but—Mrs. Warrender, he *didn't* kill himself, and they're trying to make me say he did ! "

" What ? " said Mrs. Warrender. The world seemed to be turning upside down again.

" He didn't ! I mean, he couldn't have. Oh, please, will you come and see me ? I must talk to somebody, and—you did like him, didn't you ? The night we came over to your place ? "

" I thought he was one of the most charming people I had ever met," said Mrs. Warrender sincerely. " It's terrible."

" Then you'll come. Please ! " Florence's voice cut her short. " Believe me, I'd come to you, but I daren't. If you could get over to Wright's this evening about half-past six, and we could go to my room. . . . Oh, *please*. I daren't go on talking, or somebody will hear."

" Yes, of course I will," Mrs. Warrender said, startled by the urgency of the strained voice at the other end of the 'phone. For a time she sat in her chair motionless ; then she went to her room to tidy herself, and descended for tea on the terrace.

" James," she said to her son when he joined her, " do you think it's really certain that that poor boy committed suicide ? "

" How you do go on. Really, I didn't think you could be so interested in somebody you'd only met for a few minutes," said James. But he did not say it unkindly ; perhaps Dr. Lang had given him a hint not to be too rough. At any rate his voice was unusually gentle as he added, " I'm afraid there's very little doubt about it, my dear. Lang says it looks as though he must have taken a whacking great dose."

" But he did seem so cheerful—so almost happy—when he was over here. It seems so extraordinary."

" You only saw him for an hour or so," James reminded her. " And they go up and down very quickly, change a lot, when they're like that. Besides, you don't know what happened after he left here. Somthing may have turned up to upset him."

" But I can't think what it could have been," Mrs. Warrender murmured.

" Well, how should you ? You didn't know him. I can think of half a dozen things it might have been, if you ask me."

" What ? "

" Well, suppose he found he'd got himself into trouble with that girl he was dancing with. It's common talk that he made a lot of quite unsuitable fuss about her, and a girl in her position's very likely to fasten on a fool of a young man who looks as though he has money. Suppose she suddenly cut up nasty ? Don't look like that ; I dare say it does shock you, but people do do that sort of thing, you know. And you asked me about it—I wasn't going to have told you."

" It wasn't that, quite," said Mrs. Warrender. " But, James, even if he did—die of poisoning, it needn't have been suicide, need it ? Surely people do, accidentally, take too much ? "

" If Lang's right in what he says, you can put that clean out of your head," her son replied. " Nobody would take as huge a shot as he thinks it was, by mistake. No, if you're determined to say he didn't do it himself, you'll have to think of somebody who did it for him. Murder, in fact. And murder with a hypodermic."

C

V

MRS. WARRENDER, although she had a son who was a well-known detective, had never succeeded in accustoming herself to the terms and processes of the law ; and the calm way in which James let fall the word " murder " had given her a shock—more particularly because of the introduction, in the same conversation, of suggestions about the relationships between the Haydon boy and Florence Truman. She was feeling very nervous, and in doubt what to say, as she made her way to the lounge of Wright's Hotel, where Florence, who had obviously been waiting anxiously for her to appear, beckoned her hastily out and led the way to a small uncomfortable bedroom on the top floor where the westering sun streamed uncomfortably in. She looked more white and more strained, if possible, than in the short glimpse at lunch-time, and was clearly on the verge of a breakdown. But her first words cleared up at least one complication.

" There's one thing," she began, locking the door of the little room on them, and standing with her chin held high, " that I'd like to say to you before anything else. I know what everybody's saying about this—that Jeremy killed himself because he'd been making passes at me, and I'd fallen for him and was trying to make things difficult. It isn't true."

" But, my dear," said Mrs. Warrender, hoping she had successfully suppressed her start of surprise, " why ? Why should anybody say anything so unkind ? "

" Oh, it's obvious," the girl said, with a curl of her lip. " Because he was decent and friendly to me—and you know it doesn't pay to be ' too free with the servants '—they think you mean more than you do and begin to take liberties. I'm sorry," seeing her guest's expression of distress. " I didn't mean to bother you. I don't really mind ; it's the kind of thing some people always say in places like this, when a man treats a hired dancer like me as if she was a human creature. But I'd like *you* to know it wasn't true. I wasn't making love to him and I wasn't trying to get hold of him in any way. I—I was fond of him ; he was damned decent to me, and I'd cry my eyes out now if I thought it would be any sort of good to him. He was a *nice* lad : he got one, like that. But there wasn't a single thing more to it. You believe that, don't you ? "

" Indeed ! " said Mrs. Warrender, though she did not feel quite certain whether it was a denial or a renunciation to which she had listened. " Indeed I do. But, are you sure— that he—didn't——"

" Not on your life," Florence said. " Matter of fact, I don't think he'd ever fallen for a woman at all. I believe, if you ask me, that he'd got so fed up with girls throwing themselves at his head because he was good-looking and splashed his money about that he just wasn't having any. I think he cared for his sister more than for any creature in the world—at any rate "—she turned her back and swallowed for a second—" he certainly wasn't in love with me, though he did talk to me a bit about himself now and again— more than he did to any of the lot here. That's why."

" Why what ? "

" Oh, don't you *see* ? " Florence turned and faced her. " I thought—when we met you the other night—that you sounded as if you knew about knowing people. I mean . . . you were telling us about Gladys and the silver and how you knew what had happened because you knew what sort of things Gladys could do and what she couldn't. You see what I mean ? . . . Well, I *did* know Jeremy, and I do know that he wouldn't—couldn't kill himself. Especially not now."

" Not on purpose," Mrs. Warrender said. " But couldn't he have done it accidentally ? " She was still clinging to her small hope, the more so since Florence seemed to have no suspicion of the possibility of murder.

" Accidentally ? How do you mean ? He got a great shot of morphia out of a hypodermic."

" Yes, but . . . Isn't it easy to take too much sometimes ? "

" *Sometimes* ? What do you mean ? . . . Oh ! Are people saying that—that Jeremy was a morphia addict ? "

Mrs. Warrender gave an infinitesimal nod.

" It's a lie ! It's a *damned* lie ! He never drugged in his life. I ought to know all about addicts, living in places like this, and I tell you he never did ! Besides, if you don't believe me, you've only to ask the doctor. If Jeremy had been in the habit of dosing himself with morphia out of a hypodermic, do you know what his skin would have been like ? All over punctures. And I've seen him bathing often enough—he hadn't a mark on his body."

" He hadn't got diabetes, had he or anything like that ? " Mrs. Warrender asked.

" Diabetes ? No, I'm sure he hadn't. He was as fit as anything. But why on earth——? "

" Oh, just something I thought of," said Mrs. Warrender, looking rather puzzled. There was a minute's silence. " But there was something you were going to tell me—some reason why you know he couldn't have killed himself," she said.

" Yes. . . . Only I don't quite know how to start," said Florence. " Because, you see, I'm quite certain that, apart from that, he couldn't. He wasn't that kind—he was too happy, and—and, sort of damn-it-all, something will turn up. I *know*, but I know nobody will believe me—it's just know-ing, and who takes any notice of that ? "

" It's what matters, though," said Mrs. Warrender. The girl gave her a grateful look.

" Well, anyway, look here. He *was* bothered, this last

day or two, and he did tell me about it. It was about his sister. I told you I thought he always cared for his sister more than for any other woman—well, what he told me was that his sister'd got married, a few years ago, to a fellow whom he simply couldn't stand and thought was a real bad hat ; only he was only a kid at the time—she's older than him—and he couldn't do anything about it.

"After a while his sister began to find out about her husband—but kept it to herself. It wasn't till the other day, when he got a letter from her, that he realised that it had been merry hell for her for months back, but she hadn't said a thing. In fact, she'd only written to him when she did because she'd made up her mind to try and get a divorce, and the man she'd married had rushed off round the world or something like that, and she thought she might as well use the chance to talk about it a bit. She's the kind, I understand, that would go on sticking rather anything than have a row in the home—there's a baby, you see, and all that sort of thing."

Mrs. Warrender, having the gift of silence, made no superfluous comment. The girl went on, jerkily.

"So she'd just written asking him if he'd please come home before Maurice—that's the husband—got back. They're orphans, you see, without anybody to go to except some sort of old trustee who'd let anything pass rather than have a fuss. And she asked him, *please*—like that—to come back on the next boat, and he couldn't."

"Because he'd got no money ? " Mrs. Warrender hazarded.

"Because he hadn't a bean ! Because he'd been letting a whole lot of cheap skates sponge on him here, and because a fellow he'd lent nearly all his last quarter's allowance to, and who'd solemnly promised to let him have it back three months ago, hadn't let him have a farthing. That's why he was so miserable underneath—why some people thought him a moody neurotic. He *wanted* to get back to England, to see if there wasn't a chance of making things all right for his sister before this Maurice man could get back."

" So he was really worried ? " Mrs. Warrender spoke quietly.

" Yes, fearfully. He was talking to me about it two nights ago, the evening we met you at the Grand—wondering if the man he'd lent the money to wouldn't pay by the next post, or if he could squeeze the bank for a bit extra, if he told them all about it—only he didn't want to have to, because of his sister. But he said, if everything went wrong, he'd stow away on one of the Union Castle liners, and work his passage back, because there wasn't anywhere they could put him off till Southampton. Or he'd get a passage on a yacht that wanted an extra hand—he thought he'd rather like that. Oh, don't you *see* ? " said Florence Truman. " I mean, he wasn't a bit in despair, as that beast Lewis was trying to make me say. He didn't for a minute think he wasn't going to get there somehow, only he was bothered because he didn't see how to do it without getting into an awful tangle. Only he'd never, never have just faded out and left his sister to tackle it all alone. I mayn't know much, but I do know that ! "

She stopped, and there was silence for two full minutes. Then she turned suddenly on Mrs. Warrender. " Say something, can't you ? Say that I'm a liar, and you don't believe a word I say. Only do say something ! "

" My dear, I do believe you," Mrs. Warrender said gently. " Only, I was just thinking——"

" What ? "

" Sit down," said Mrs. Warrender ; and, somewhat to her surprise, the girl sat. " You see, I'm quite sure you're telling me the truth, and I think you know a great deal about Mr. Haydon, because you were so fond of him. No, dear, I don't mean anything you wouldn't like me to mean, and anyhow I think affection gives one a great deal clearer insight into people than just falling in love—I'm afraid I don't express myself very well, but perhaps you see what I mean. I'm sure you know, if you say Mr. Haydon wasn't going to kill himself. But if he wasn't, and you say he couldn't have killed himself by accident—wait a moment, dear—don't you see, somebody must have killed him? "

" I don't. . . . You mean, he was *murdered*? " Florence Truman said.

" That's what my son said, this afternoon, and he's got a great deal of experience. He said, ' if he didn't do it himself, you'll have to think of somebody who did it for him.' My *dear*, don't ! "

" I wasn't. I'm not going to cry. Only," said Florence, " I never thought of it. Do you mean—somebody *murdered* Jeremy ? Killed him, like that ? "

" It's dreadful, I know," said Mrs. Warrender. " Only— I don't see anything else."

" If they did," said the girl, clenching her thin hands very slowly and staring until her eyes came out of her head, " I won't do a thing else—I won't eat or sleep or do anything, until I've made them pay for it. It—it's like killing a baby, to hurt anything as decent and happy as Jeremy. Don't you think so ? " Mrs. Warrender nodded.

Florence Truman walked up and down the room for a few seconds, muttering a little to herself. Then she turned and faced her visitor. " You're right," she said. " You must be right. God knows why I didn't think of it myself, only I was a fool and got into a rage. He *was* murdered. *Jeremy Haydon was murdered.* . . . Listen." She stood, staring straight at Mrs. Warrender, and spoke in a low determined voice. " I swear—now—by Almighty God, that, if it costs me all I have and all I hope for, I will see that his murderers are punished. But," she added, " you've got to help me."

" I ! But, dear——"

" Don't you see," said Florence, in the same quiet tone,

" there are just the two of us, you and I, who know that he was murdered. I know because I know he couldn't have killed himself, and you know because you believed me when I said so and because you saw that there was nothing else that could have happened. But nobody else knows it except us two. Lewis, and the doctor, and his bank, they all believe he killed himself—and I'll bet anything your son thinks so too, doesn't he? . . . I thought as much. So, you see, they won't do anything about it—they'll just have an inquest and bury him quick out of the way, so that Lewis won't lose his summer visitors, and it'll all be forgotten, and if I say anything, I'll be fired, and that'll be that. Oh, don't you understand? You *can't* do nothing ; you couldn't go home when your holiday's over and know he'd been murdered and you hadn't said a word. You might meet his sister some day in England—I met her once. And he was nice to you, wasn't he? It isn't for me I'm asking. It's because we're the only two who *know*."

" My dear," said Mrs. Warrender, very much moved, " of course I'll do anything I can to help. But what *can* an old lady like me do? "

" I don't know." The light faded out of Florence's eyes, and she dropped into a chair. " I don't know what either of us can do, really. But there is—there must be *something*."

" You see," said Mrs. Warrender, picking her words slowly, " if he was really killed, it must have been—he must have been killed by somebody. And the question is— who? "

" Yes," Florence echoed dully. " *Who*? "

" ' A murderer—with a hypodermic,' " Mrs. Warrender quoted, half under her breath. " My dear, what is it? " For Florence had stiffened and was staring at her as if she had seen a ghost.

" My heavens, do you know everything? That girl—the

one you saw—Clare Ferrers—and her boy friend—they dope like fiends. How did you know?"

"I didn't," said Mrs. Warrender. "It was only something my son said."

"She'd have enough morphia to sink a battleship. But I don't know why she should want to kill him. She sucked him dry. I'd have killed *her* half a dozen times for the asking. She didn't like his consorting with the lower classes," Florence said bitterly. She paused a moment, and an ugly look came over her face. "If it was, I'll—I'll jolly well have the hide off her! She's going to get what's coming to her some day, anyhow, the mean, spiteful little——"

"Please! Just a minute," Mrs. Warrender interrupted. "I mean—we mustn't be in too much of a hurry, must we?" She hesitated, putting her thought into shape. "You see, my dear, it's a question of what we *know*, isn't it, just as you said? I *knew* about Gladys, and you *know* about Mr. Haydon —I think you're right, I think I would have known too, if I'd seen a little more of him. Now, you know these friends of his you were talking about, and I've only seen two of them and that just for two minutes. So I must rely on you. Do you know—do you think, quite honestly—that one of them, Miss Ferrers, perhaps, would be a—murderer? It's very important, you see, to be quite certain. Lots of people can be very unpleasant and not be murderers."

Florence looked up quickly, and flushed a little.

"Meaning, don't be a cat, and let your private spites come in. I get you. . . . No-o. I suppose, if I'm being honest," she said reluctantly. "I don't see Clare Ferrers murdering anybody. I hate her like poison, but, as you say, that's not the point. And if she wasn't, there isn't any one of them that would. They're a poor greedy sponging lot—and I know some of them pretty well, a lot better, really, than Jeremy did. But I *don't* feel they're murderers. That's a lot of help, isn't it?"

"Well, then," said Mrs. Warrender, "it was somebody else."

"But who? *Who*? That's what I can't think. He didn't know anybody else, unless you count barmen and shopkeepers down the town, and the bank manager, but why should they kill him? Unless you're going to say there was a lunatic walking around."

"I don't think lunatics generally have hypodermics full of morphia," said Mrs. Warrender.

"I suppose they don't—anyway there aren't any here, that I'm aware of. Why did you want to know if Jeremy had diabetes, by the way?"

"Only a funny little thing I noticed," said Mrs. Warrender. "You know, it was I who picked up the syringe." She screwed up her eyes for a moment, the recollection of that scene was still too near the surface of consciousness. "I happened to notice the name on it, because it was my own chemists—Loxley's in Baker Street. They're very good, but they're not a big firm, and I should be very surprised if you could buy one of their hypodermics in Funchal."

"What difference does it make where it was bought?"

"Don't you see, dear, if Mr. Haydon had had one of his own—if he'd been in the habit of taking morphia—or if he'd had diabetes or anything you have to take injections for—he might quite likely have bought the syringe in London. But you tell me he didn't——"

"And I'll swear that's true."

"I'm sure you're right, my dear. Well, if he hadn't got one, and had suddenly decided to commit suicide, he might have bought one in the town, but I'm sure it wouldn't have been one from Loxley's. So it looks as though it might have been somebody else's."

"That's clever of you," the girl said, rather wearily; "but I don't see that it gets us anywhere much. Unless it means that we should look for a homicidal lunatic, who had a syringe from Baker Street, and hasn't got it now."

" I don't think it could have been a homicidal lunatic," Mrs. Warrender said. " I'm sure Mr. Haydon wouldn't have waited while a strange madman stuck a syringe into him. He'd have fought him. It must have been someone he knew quite well. Someone he knew but you didn't, perhaps."

Florence shook her head.

" Oh, but, my dear, you didn't know everybody he knew. You weren't with him all the time." Mrs. Warrender's voice was gentle. " For instance, the day before he died—what was he doing then ? "

" I don't really know. I didn't see much of him that day. He was out somewhere a good bit of the time."

" With his friends ? "

" No. They'd all gone off in a car somewhere. I think myself he was glad to be shut of them for a bit."

" Then he might have met somebody. Look here," said Mrs. Warrender, " don't you feel that's what we ought to do ? Try to find out what he was doing the day before, and see whether that doesn't tell us anything ? "

" It wasn't the day before ; matter of fact, it was the same day."

" Oh ! " Mrs. Warrender had forgotten, for the moment, Dr. Lang's words.

" I heard the doctor saying to one of the policemen, ' between ten and twelve last night.' Anyway, his bed wasn't slept in. He must have been lying out there all night. That's one of the things that's sickening to think of, though I suppose it doesn't matter to him. You die pretty quickly of a shot of morphia, don't you ? "

" I'm sure you don't feel or notice anything," Mrs. War- render reassured her. " But isn't it queer that nobody noticed him there ? "

" Not so much as you'd think. People lie there all day, off and on. They turn over, of course, and oil themselves ;

but unless you were looking you would quite likely not notice if they didn't. And his place was right at the end, and he never cared much to talk to people while he was sunbathing. If you hadn't come this morning, I expect he'd be there now —or until something or somebody noticed him," said Florence with a shudder.

"My dear, you mustn't!" Mrs. Warrender turned pale, finding that others could imagine large white birds with beaks. "Don't—we *can't* stop to think of horrors."

"Sorry," said the girl. "Maybe I'm going crazy."

"We know," Mrs. Warrender went on, in the desire to shut out visions thinking with a rapidity unusual to her, "we know that he was killed by the pool sometime between ten and twelve."

"Perhaps he wasn't killed there."

"Oh, I think he must have been. I'm sure nobody would have tried to carry a big man like Mr. Haydon—and in a bathing-suit. They would have been sure to be seen. I wonder if anyone did see them—or see Mr. Haydon down there? Was he in the hotel for dinner, do you know?"

"Yes, I saw him. But he went upstairs pretty soon, and then I didn't see him again."

"Would anybody have been likely to see him down there? At about ten or eleven?"

"Not very likely," the girl said, "unless they'd been bathing, and I shouldn't think it was very likely that anyone was. You see, it was gala night at your hotel, and you've got a big pool, so most of our people would have gone there, if they wanted to bathe. The hotels take turns for gala nights."

"Still he *was* bathing, so I suppose the other person probably was too, and somebody might have seen them. I wonder if he had a visitor that evening. No, that was silly of me. Anybody who wanted to murder him wouldn't come walking up to the door and ask for him. I wonder if he'd made an appointment with the other man."

" You seem very sure there *was* another man."

" But, of course, there must have been. Or else he couldn't have been killed, could he ? " said Mrs. Warrender. She wrinkled her brows. " Did he have a letter, or a note or anything, in the morning, do you know ? "

" I don't. But I should think the porter would. I could ask him."

" If he had, and he didn't throw it away, it would be in his rooms, or his clothes, I suppose."

" They won't let you in to look there. I tried and they threw me out," said Florence.

" Or he may have had an appointment when he went down to the town. I do wonder where he went. You're sure you haven't any idea ? "

" I don't *know* where he went, of course. But if he did what he ordinarily did, I know where he might have been part of the time."

" Where ? "

" At that big café—Joao's, it's called ; I don't know if you know it—down on the waterfront, just opposite the jetty where the launches land."

" Yes, I know it. With the big awnings, and the golden sun on top of it."

" That's right. Well, Jeremy used to go into Joao's in the afternoon, practically every day that he was down in the town, and sit there often quite a long time looking at the harbour. He was great pals with a waiter there, a nice lad called Tomas, and they used to have long talks."

" So, if he'd been going to meet anybody, he might have met them there. . . . Does Mr. Tomas speak any English ? "

" Oh, yes. Badly, but he does speak it. Otherwise, Jeremy wouldn't have been able to talk to him—he was just lazy about learning foreign languages. I once or twice helped him out with some Portuguese, because I pick lingoes up like a monkey. But with Tomas it really wasn't necessary. Why ? "

" Well, I thought perhaps he would know and could tell us if Mr. Haydon met anybody there yesterday."

" Do you mean go and ask him ? "

Mrs. Warrender nodded.

" What, now ? "

Mrs. Warrender looked at her watch, and gave a little squeal. " My dear, I'm so sorry ! I'd no idea it was so late. And, of course, you've got to go on duty."

" I didn't mean that. I needn't go on till nine o'clock, and anyhow it doesn't matter much to me now. If old Lewis gives me any of his lip, I'll tell him to go and fry himself in his own fat—I expect he's intending to give me the sack anyway. I was thinking of you. Oughtn't you to go back and have some dinner ? Wouldn't be any good to have you knocking yourself up."

" I don't feel I want any dinner. I had a good tea, and I'm not really very hungry in the evenings," Mrs. Warrender said. " I would *much* rather go on and find out something, if there is anything to find out. But I think perhaps, if I'm not going back, I ought to send a message to my son, or he might be worrying. Perhaps I could telephone—or get somebody to telephone for me "—Mrs. Warrender had never got over her fear of telephones, and foreign telephones were particularly terrifying—" just so that he knows I'm all right. I expect you could find me a little something to eat when we've finished ? That is, if you are sure you really ought to manage it. I would much rather have somebody with me than go and talk to Mr. Tomas all alone ; but I shouldn't like you to lose your post."

" My post, as you call it, isn't worth worrying about. I'll lose it now or at the end of the season, and I can't say I care which," the girl said listlessly. " I'll come along if you like ; it's better than doing nothing and wondering what people are saying. Let's go, shall we ? "

" You haven't got a—a photograph of Mr. Haydon

anywhere, have you ? " asked Mrs. Warrender. She was not at all sure why she should ask for a photograph ; but she had a vague idea that detectives always carried photographs about with them.

"As it happens, I've got a nice one, though it's only a snap," Florence said. " Here it is. You can have it if you like. I'd like to have it back some time, though."

" Of *course*, dear. Of course you shall," said Mrs. Warrender, stowing the print away in her handbag.

" Did you say you wanted to telephone ? "

" I think—I think I'd like to ask Dr. Lang to send a message, if we could find his room," Mrs. Warrender said. Florence stared a little, but prepared to comply. She was not aware that Mrs. Warrender's investigation of her handbag had discovered yet another reason for consulting Dr. Lang. James, alleging that she always muddled the change, hardly ever let her have any money, and she was sure, though she did not know the market rate for information in Madeira, that detectives always had to pay for it. And of course Florence mustn't be allowed to pay, even if she had the money, which was very unlikely.

So, guided by Florence, she came to the door of the Langs' suite, and was very much relieved to find Dr. Lang himself in the corridor about ten yards off. It was much easier to ask him questions when Persis's roaring geniality was not within hearing. Trying very hard, but without much success, not to seem agitated, she explained that she was staying to have dinner with Miss Truman, and would Dr. Lang be so very kind as to telephone a message to James, because she couldn't manage the telephone ? And further, would Dr. Lang be even more kind, and lend her five pounds in Portuguese currency. (She thought that should cover contingencies, not realising how joyfully any Madeiran would leap at a handful of British small change.) For she had stupidly come out without any, and would want some after dinner. The doctor looked at her for an instant, but immediately produced the funds requested.

Then, trying to make her voice sound only like that of an inquisitive tourist, she said, " Oh, Dr. Lang ! You saw poor Mr. Haydon, didn't you ? Can you tell me—could it be true what they're saying ? That he'd take a lot of drugs, often— I mean, that he was in the habit of it ? "

" Not by injection, he didn't," the doctor said, " and you can tell anybody that you like. Of course, if he'd swallowed them or sniffed cocaine, say, that wouldn't show. But I'd be prepared to bet he didn't ; looked a thoroughly healthy fellow."

" Oh, I'm so glad," said Mrs. Warrender. " What——" she tried to find a plausible way of disguising her question, and gave it up—" I wonder what happened to the syringe."

" The police, or whatever they call themselves here, took it with the bottle you found. I suppose they're keeping it somewhere," said Dr. Lang, lifting his eyebrows a trifle. " Come in and see Persis, won't you, if you're not in a hurry. She was resting, but she'll be up now."

" Oh, thank you very much, but I *really* must go ; I'll be keeping Miss Truman waiting," said Mrs. Warrender ; and fled. If he thought her an elderly ghoul she could not help it. Actually, Dr. Lang stared after her for a minute or two in indecision. She looked, he thought, rather queer and over-excited ; and he was sure that it would not be good for her to be in the company of that dancing girl, who was probably pretty much upset herself, poor thing.

VI

MRS. WARRENDER found her way back to Florence, and so to the hotel entrance, where, feeling unusually competent, she hailed a taxi to take them to the waterfront. They spoke little on the way down. Florence seemed sunk in her thoughts, and Mrs. Warrender, beyond one timid pat on her knee, refrained from interrupting.

When they reached Joao's, on the waterfront, Florence appeared suddenly to wake up, and to begin to take command. "I'll tell you what we're going to do," she said, "we're going to sit down and order omelettes, before we even try to get hold of Tomas. It's quite silly, your thinking you can go and talk to people without having anything to eat, and I haven't been sacked yet—I've got enough for that."

"Oh, my dear—but I couldn't *dream* of letting you pay. I've got *heaps* of money," said Mrs. Warrender, displaying it proudly. "I thought we might need some for Mr. Tomas. So I borrowed it."

Florence laughed—Mrs. Warrender had not heard her laugh for forty-eight hours.

"You really are a darling," she said. "Tomas won't need tipping. But you must eat something."

"If you say so, dear," Mrs. Warrender acquiesced, and looking out towards the bay, along the short stone jetty with its groups of idle strollers. But there were no snorting little launches there to take passengers to and fro from the liners, for there was no big ship anchored there that evening. Florence secured omelettes, one of which she ate rapidly, while Mrs. Warrender picked politely at the other.

Eventually, Florence beckoned to a small waiter with a monkey-face, and said " *Deux cognacs*——"

" But please, I don't want brandy," said Mrs. Warrender.

" Then I'll drink both of them," said Florence.

When the waiter came back with the cognacs, Florence said, " Wait a minute, Tomas. You know me ? "

The man nodded.

" And you have heard—what's happened ? "

" Oh, si ! Yahs, yess. It is veree sad, yahs ? " He really did look distressed, even if his English was not equal to the occasion.

" It is. It was so—sudden," said Florence, with a wry face. " You saw him yesterday, perhaps ? He went to the town."

" Yes, indeed I see him. He was having his drink here, like always, and I serve him, yahs, like always."

" What time ? "

" But I do not know. The same time, like always."

" Was he with a friend ? "

" Oh, no," said Tomas. Their faces fell. " Indeed, no. I know his friends well indeed. He was not a friend, no."

" What ? " Both spoke simultaneously, but Mrs. Warrender yielded.

" He did have somebody with him then ? " Florence said.

" Oh, yahs. But not his friend."

" Who was it ? "

" Oh, I do not know. It was a man. He come walking past, and he say, ' Fahnsee you here,' and the señor say, ' Yes, I am here, like always. You have a drink, yes—no ? ' So they have two—three."

"You didn't hear what they said?" Mrs. Warrender intervened.

"Yahs. Some I hear. But not understand. I understand ze English only so, when I listen, like always." Tomas smiled ingratiatingly.

"And you weren't listening then."

"No. I have many peoples, because of the big ship. I cannot listen. I only hear when zey say, 'Well, so long. Ten-thirty at ze hotel.' Pardon, senora, they call me," and Tomas shot away, unaware of the sensation his words had made.

"You were right." Florence stared at Mrs. Warrender. "And I thought you were dreaming. He *did* meet somebody here, somebody I didn't know——"

"By chance, you know," replied Mrs. Warrender. "He said, 'Fancy seeing you here.'"

"And he was going to meet him again, at Wright's, at ten-thirty. Oh, Lord," said Florence, "you're a witch. Look here, let's pay Tomas—I think he gets double tip, don't you? —and go back. Can you run to another taxi?"

"If he came," said Mrs. Warrender in the taxi—she was now nearly as excited as her companion—"how did he get in, without being seen? You said Mr. Haydon hadn't had any visitors."

"Oh, I suppose Jeremy walked up the drive and met him. Or he could have come in at the side-entrance—that's not locked till ten forty-five. But what could he do when he got there?" Her eyes were shining, and her lips moving; she looked a different girl.

"Bathe," said Mrs. Warrender. "Mr. Haydon was bathing."

"Oh, yes. He might have gone straight to the pool, of course. But how do we know?"

"What do you do when you bathe?" Mrs. Warrender asked.

" Why, undress, I suppose."

" Yes, but then ? I mean, I'm sorry if I'm putting it stupidly ; but, if Mr. Haydon wanted a bathing-suit and a towel, where would he get it from ? "

" From his locker."

" And if his friend did too—I mean, people don't generally come out in the evening carrying bathing-suits, do they ? "

" He'd have to get one out of the store. Oh, I see ! . . . No." Florence's face clouded over. " I'm afraid that's a wash-out. You see, there's somebody on duty at the store most of the day, but he goes off at ten, unless it's a gala night. And the residents have keys, in case they might want to entertain a friend suddenly. So Jeremy would just have had to unlock the door, and fish a costume out, and nobody would have known.

" What is odder," she said, after a pause, " is how on earth the man got out again."

" Why ? "

" Well, if he came in through the side-gate, okay. But that gate's locked at 10-45, and unless he'd been very quick, he couldn't have bathed *and* killed Jeremy and got up again, all in a quarter of an hour, could he ? "

" Couldn't he have gone straight out, by the ordinary way ? "

" We-ell. There's a man on there, every night, to check up who comes in and who goes out. They had some sort of row with the police, I believe ; and that was why they put him on. Anyway he was there. Besides, you think the man came incog., don't you ? So he wouldn't want to go away in a blaze of publicity. But how on earth *did* he get away ? "

By now there were at the entrance to Wright's Hotel.

" I think I'll go down to the pool store," Florence said. " It isn't ten yet, and Jose's rather a friend of mine. I might get something out of him. Will you wait here? "

"No, I think I'll come down with you," said Mrs. Warrender. "It will be cooler by the pool, and I would like to know if you find out anything."

While Florence went to talk to the bathing attendant, Mrs. Warrender proceeded down the farthest flight of steps which led to the pool itself, and stood for a long time at the point on its rim where a stairway led down to a rope-ladder which in turn led down to the sea. Across the still black water the lights of Funchal pricked the darkness.

"Mrs. Warrender! Mrs. Warrender!" Florence, all excited, came springing down the steps to her. "José doesn't know about anybody having bathed last night. But, what do you think, he's lost a bathing-costume out of the store! And he knows it was there yesterday. What's that mean? But you aren't listening!"

"Yes, I am, dear," said Mrs. Warrender. "But just come here for a minute." She took her to the lip of the pool, and pointed to where, very near owing to the curve of the bay, the bathing-pool of the Grand Hotel projected into the sea. "I shouldn't think the Grand Hotel pool is as much as a quarter of a mile from here, and look how beautifully calm it is. If he was a good swimmer, he could make his own clothes into a bundle, and swim there carrying them, and nobody would ever know he'd been here."

"My God! And then he'd go back and mix with the Grand Hotel crowd." Florence stared across the motionless water.

"You remember it was a gala night," said Mrs. Warrender. "There would be quite a lot of people there. I think, my dear, we'd better walk over to the Grand Hotel, don't you? It isn't far, if you can spare the time."

"What shall we do there?"

" Oh, see if we can find his bathing-dress. I don't suppose he would have wanted to keep it longer than he needed, do you ? "

When they had reached the Grand Hotel, Mrs. Warrender led the way to the bathing-pool, and inquired, in her gentlest voice, of the attendant on duty whether she could be allowed to have the keys of all the bathing boxes.

" *All*, madam ? " asked he, surprised.

" Well, you see," said Mrs. Warrender, " we think we may have left a bathing-dress in one of them, and we can't remember which. What colour was it, dear ? "

" Orange," said Florence.

" There *was* an orange bathing-dress found this morning, in Number 51, but I am afraid it wasn't yours. It belonged to Wright's Hotel. So we're sending it back there. I'm sorry."

" But it might have been—thank you so much—it might have been the one I mean. My friend didn't say where he'd got it," said Mrs. Warrender, " only where he'd left it, and he might have come over from Wright's."

" Perhaps in the boat," the official agreed. " I saw people were using the boat last night."

" Boat ? " said Florence.

" There's a boat just by the pool, miss. People use it to row out to that island. Anybody can use it, if they know how to undo it."

" If you haven't actually sent back the bathing-dress, might I see it ? " said Mrs. Warrender. " I might just know, from looking, whether it was the one my friend was wearing —he's the kind of man who would never know where it came from." And, as he turned to get it, she whispered rapidly to Miss Truman, " Look at it all you can, my dear ; you may be able to notice something."

" I didn't get anything but its number, which may be worth knowing," Florence Truman said. " But, honestly, you're a living marvel. I didn't believe a bit in this other man when you suggested him, but now you've not only proved that he existed, but that he swam over from Wright's last evening——"

" Rowed, dear," said Mrs. Warrender. " Much quicker, and less splashy. It was silly of me not to think of it before."

" What do we do now, then ? "

" I suppose," said Mrs. Warrender, " we go up to the hotel, and see whether there is anyone staying there who would possibly fit."

Her voice faltered a little on the last words ; it was a long pull up from the pool to the hotel, and she suddenly felt very tired. But Florence Truman was buoyant.

" Ends of the earth, if you say so," she said. " Gosh, but you don't know what a difference all this makes ! It's like being in a new world. Hi, don't trip over the cobbles."

They arrived, at length, in the foyer of the Grand Hotel, and casually inspected the register. But they found nothing of interest.

" There's nobody arrived at all," said Mrs. Warrender. " But I'm sure, from the way Tomas was talking, that this man had only just come."

" Then he must have come on that German boat, the day before," Florence observed. " There's no English liner calling round about now—What's the matter ? "

" Oh, but I'm so *silly* ! " Mrs. Warrender exclaimed. " The *Armadilla*—that big cruising ship. If you please "— she addressed the porter, with some little difficulty, because he seemed to have turned into two or three porters, and it was so awkward not to know which one you ought to look at—" could you tell me what time the *Armadilla* left, yesterday ? And where was she going ? "

" She left at twelve-thirty, madam," said the porter. " Making for Buenos Aires."

" Oh ? And passengers went ashore ? "

" Oh, yes, madam, quite a lot. The launches were running quite late, taking them back."

" Launches. We ought to go and see all the l-launches," said Mrs. Warrender ; and suddenly collapsed in a small heap on the floor.

VII

MRS. WARRENDER woke the next morning from a long and sound sleep, with the feeling that one occasionally has that something important has happened, but one cannot imagine what it is.

She lay still, slowly collecting her wits, and wondering a little why she felt so limp. Then her eye was caught by her clothes, lying on a chair, and she looked at them again in mild perplexity. What had she been thinking of, to leave them like that when she came to bed? Reflecting on this, she was surprised to find that she had no recollection of taking off her clothes when she came to bed, or, indeed, of coming to bed at all. Now how could that be? At this point in her reflections there was a knock on the door, and James came in.

" Good-morning, dear," said Mrs. Warrender cheerfully. " It looks like another nice day. Why, James, is anything the matter? You look quite worried."

" I should think so ! " her son burst out. " What do you suppose, when you gave us such a fright last night? Going and fainting in the foyer, with everybody looking at you ! " He said the last words with indignation, as though the publicity added to the offence.

" Oh ! " It all began to come back. Joao's, the pool, the orange bathing-dress, and asking about the sailing-time of the *Armadilla*. And, of course, she had been meaning to find out about the launches. Mrs. Warrender sat up in bed with a feeling of determination. What a pity she had been so foolish as to faint, and to cause James, doubtless, a lot of inconvenience.

" I *am* so sorry, dear," she said. " It was *very* silly of me, and so tiresome for you. It was nothing—only that I was a little tired——"

" No wonder, going all over the place with that girl, and having practically no dinner ! " James said. " If Lang hadn't happened to be over here, I should have had to get some dago doctor from the hotel ! But he carried you up, and we 'phoned for his wife to come over and put you to bed, and Lang gave you a sleeping-draught."

" Oh, dear, what a nuisance I've been ! And a sleeping-draught too ! That must be why I slept so soundly. I feel *perfectly* well now," Mrs. Warrender said.

" That's as may be. But you'll stop in bed to-day and have no gallivanting about," said James severely.

" Yes, dear," meekly. " Do you know what happened to Miss Truman ? "

" I don't. I gave her a piece of my mind, and packed her off to her own place. And I hope the manager ticked her off properly. Pure selfishness ! " said James. His mother gave a small sigh, but was too experienced to attempt a defence. " Well, mother, shall I ring for your breakfast ? "

" If you please, dear. Oh, James," as he turned to go, " I wonder if you could spare me a little time. I've something rather important I want to ask you."

" If you want to, by all means. I suppose this afternoon would do ; I must do some work now. Mind, you're not to get up to-day—Lang says so."

" No, dear. Thank you very much." Poor James, his case seemed to be very troublesome.

During the interval, while she was waiting for her breakfast and eating it, Mrs. Warrender strove to set her recollections in order. Jeremy Haydon had met a man in the town on the afternoon of his death, a stranger to the place, and one who seemed surprised to see him. He had made an appointment with this man at Wright's Hotel for ten-thirty that evening, and by midnight, at latest, he was dead—in his bathing-suit. This, she said to herself, was quite certain, quite proved. Then there was the rest, which she believed was certain but which James would certainly say was not proved ; that the unknown came to Wright's not by land, but in the boat from the Grand Hotel's bathing-pool, that he bathed in an orange bathing-dress taken by Jeremy from the store at Wright's, and that he subsequently, having killed Jeremy, rowed back to the Grand Hotel and dressed, leaving his borrowed bathing-dress in one of their boxes.

Why not dress before he went back ? Because, Mrs. Warrender argued to herself, somebody *might* have turned up any moment, and he have been seen. Then—it must be true—he had hurried down to the harbour and got on a launch going to the *Armadilla*, and was now on his way to Buenos Aires—the cruel, callous brute ! But—who *was* he ? And why did he want to murder Jeremy Haydon ?

What could she do ? She could try and find out if a strange man had gone away late on a launch, though she had hoped that James would do that for her. It was so difficult, not knowing at all what he looked like. Of course, she might ask Tomas that. Or she could take the photograph of Jeremy, which Florence had given to her, and see whether anybody—the bank manager, perhaps—had seen him about with a strange man.

She reached for the snapshot, which lay on the table beside her. But, when she got it, she found to her surprise that it was two snapshots, which must have got stuck together. The top one was of Jeremy Haydon, leaning against the rail of the pool and drinking a long drink. The other was of a group : Jeremy, a woman looking rather like him, but a few years older, and another man. Mrs. Warrender stared long and seriously at the second photograph. An idea—an idea which startled her both by its incredibility and by the way in which it seemed to fit—had come to her. She put the photograph down and got out of bed with determination.

For James's instructions she had ceased to care; this was life or death.

She dressed, feeling a little more shaky than she would have liked to own, and made her way downstairs. There she bearded the porter—who looked at her sympathetically and tried to start a conversation about the heat—and made him ring up Wright's Hotel and get Florence Truman on the telephone. For a time there was a slight confusion of courtesies, as she enquired after Florence's job and Florence expressed anxiety about her health; but at length this was resolved and she managed to put her question about the photograph.

" Oh, I didn't know you'd got it," Florence said. " It must have stuck. Yes, of course, it's him and his sister— Mrs. Benoni—and the other man's her husband."

" I thought that might be it," said Mrs. Warrender. " Tell me—I thought you said Mr. Benoni was out of England."

" So he is. Cruising somewhere, Jeremy told me. But— oh, I say—you don't think——? "

" Hush, my dear! *Don't* say anything. Not on the telephone. I will tell you, but I must think. Good-bye, my dear." And Mrs. Warrender, literally trembling with agitation, rang off.

No more delay. Regardless of the heat, and a certain inconvenient light-headedness, Mrs. Warrender found a hat, and a taxi, and set off for the town. She alighted at the offices of the firm which acted as general tourist agency for the whole of Madeira, and asked the clerk if she could see the passenger list of the *Armadilla*.

There, however, she met a check. The clerk—he was a bored, unintelligent underling—said that the passenger list of the *Armadilla* was private. She was not a liner; she was on a pleasure cruise, and it was no business of casual callers to know who was on board her.

" Oh, but it's very important to me ! I do want to know if—if a friend of mine is on her," Mrs. Warrender quavered.

" Sorry, madam. We cannot help that. I have no authority," said the clerk, and disappeared somewhere into the back of the office.

" Oh, dear ! " Mrs. Warrender sat down rather suddenly on a very worn leather seat, and looked at an advertisement of winter tours to the Amazon, wishing very much that she did not feel so inclined to cry. At this moment, the entrance door behind her opened, and an indignant bark said : " Mrs. Warrender ! What on earth are you doing down here ? Surely James told you——"

" Oh, Dr. Lang ! " Mrs. Warrender cried, forgetful of everything, but that here was a port in a storm. " Dr. Lang ! *Please* help me. The man at the counter won't let me see the passenger list of the *Armadilla*, and it's really dreadfully important that I should. Can't you make him, please, Dr. Lang ? I know you must think I've gone quite mad—but I must see it ! No, no ! " as he tried to soothe her, and take her away. " I can't help what James or you or anybody thinks. I must see that list, and I can't go away from here until I do."

An alarmed Englishman, particularly if he barks when alarmed, has a remarkable effect in Madeira ; and Dr. Lang was at the moment decidedly alarmed. He had an affection for Mrs. Warrender of which she was hardly aware ; he was genuinely distressed to see her pale face and excited eyes, and he understood that a Portuguese official was the proximate cause of them. So he banged on the counter, and bellowed at the Portuguese official in his most imperialist manner, until the latter, cowed into believing that he was about to create an " international incident," apologised and yielded up the precious document. Mrs. Warrender followed its length with a quivering finger until, with what was almost a hiccup of excitement, she found the name she sought.

" Oh, *thank* you, Dr. Lang ! " she said.

" That all you want ? And now," said the doctor, with determination, " will you please allow me to take you back to the hotel and put you straight into bed ? "

" It's so very kind of you," said Mrs. Warrender, obeying, " and I'm afraid I've been very tiresome and taken up a great deal of your time."

" Not at all. My job. But you will go and rest now, won't you ? " the doctor said.

" Oh, I will ! But—do you think you could ask James to come and see me first ? I know he's busy ; but I wouldn't keep him more than a minute or two. And I should be so much happier."

" I'll see he does," Dr. Lang promised.

In a very few minutes after their arrival at the hotel, James Warrender duly appeared, looking distinctly cross. Anxiety always made James Warrender cross.

" Well, mother, here I am," he said. " Lang said you wanted to see me."

" James, can you tell me about old Mr. Haydon's money ? "

" *Haydon's* ? Why on earth—what do you want to know ? "

" Who got it, when he died ? "

" Why, the children, so far as I know. That young chap who killed himself, and his sister."

" But to spend, did they ? I mean, I thought you told me young Mr. Haydon couldn't get at the capital. Or something like that."

" Oh, I see. Yes, I believe that was so. I'm not absolutely certain," said James, after a pause, " but I'm nearly sure they each got the interest on their share of the estate until they were twenty-five or until they married."

" And suppose one of them died ? "

" The other got the lot. I know that."

" Are you sure that they, either of them, got it all when they married ? "

" Yes, I am sure. I remember that particularly, because I thought old Haydon was a fool to put it that way. Was sure that Maurice Benoni was a scamp, and that he'd get hold of his wife's money, somehow, if it was absolutely hers. I advised the old man to tie it up on the girl and her children ; but he never listened to anything anybody said—Why ? "

" Only," said Mrs. Warrender, feeling she had at last come to the end of her nightmare, " I think Maurice Benoni must have murdered Mr. Haydon."

" *Murdered* ? My dear mother, you're mad." James Warrender looked properly scandalised at such wild leaping to conclusions.

" No, dear. You see, he was here, the other day. He came on the *Armadilla*, and I'm almost certain he met Mr. Haydon. No, dear, just a minute, I'm not being silly, if you'd only just listen." And she unfolded the story of the two days' research, ending with the discovery of the name of Maurice Benoni on the passenger list of the *Armadilla*.

" You see, dear," she finished, " I've got a photograph of him here, and I meant to have asked Mr. Tomas, the waiter, if it was the same man, only I got rather tired. But I'm quite sure, if *you* asked him, you'd find out ; and if he got back to the ship so late, just before it was going to sail, some of those men who run the launches would remember taking him. If that photograph's at all right, he must be quite a funny-looking man—the sort of person people would remember."

" I dare say," said James thoughtfully. " Yes, I'll certainly look into it. You leave it to me, mother. Don't you worry your head."

" Indeed I won't," said Mrs. Warrender. " I just—thought you'd like to—know." And, much to her subsequent shame, she then and there fell asleep.

" Not at all a bad job, though I say it as shouldn't," said James, a little while afterwards, when, after intensive enquiries, the necessary identification had been secured, and an extradition warrant issued for Maurice Benoni. " Quite sharp of you, mother, to have spotted that that syringe couldn't have been got in Madeira. I don't mind saying that had quite slipped my notice. But I think, on the whole, we didn't do too badly over that case. Of course, there's no direct money in it ; but that sort of thing rather helps. Gets you known, and all that."

" I'm so glad, dear," said Mrs. Warrender. " But, James —I'm so sorry, but I quite forgot. I borrowed five pounds from Dr. Lang and I never gave it back. Could you pay it ? I've got quite a lot of it still left, so it isn't so much as it sounds."

" *Five pounds* ? What on earth did you want five pounds for ? " said James.